VULGAR THE VIKING AND THE GREAT GULP GAMES

LOOK OUT FOR MORE STORIES OF MAYHEM AND CHAOS IN

VULGAR THE VIKING AND THE ROCK CAKE RAIDERS

VULGAR THE VIKING AND THE SPOOKY SCHOOL TRIP

VULGAR THE VIKING IN BLUBBER'S GOT TALENT!

VULGAR THE VIKING AND THE GREAT GULP GAMES

ODIN REDBEARD

ILLUSTRATED BY
SARAH HORNE

nosy
crow

With special thanks to
Barry Hutchison

First published in the UK in 2012 by Nosy Crow Ltd
The Crow's Nest, 10a Lant St
London, SE1 1QR, UK

Nosy Crow and associated logos are trademarks and/or
registered trademarks of Nosy Crow Ltd

Text copyright © Hothouse Fiction, 2012
Illustrations © Sarah Horne, 2012

The right of Hothouse Fiction and Sarah Horne to be identified as the author
and illustrator respectively of this work has been asserted by them in accordance
with the Copyright, Designs and Patents Act 1988.

A CIP catalogue record for this book will be available from the British Library

Printed and bound in the UK by Clays Ltd, St Ives Plc

Papers used by Nosy Crow are made from wood grown in sustainable forests.

ISBN: 978 0 85763 058 2

www.nosycrow.com

CHAPTER ONE

IN THE MARKET FOR A FIGHT

Vegetables. Vulgar hated vegetables.

Real Vikings shouldn't eat vegetables, he thought. *Real Vikings should eat...* well, he wasn't actually sure what real Vikings should eat, but it wasn't vegetables. Bears maybe. Or dragons.

But not cabbage. Never cabbage.

"Four cabbages," his mum, Helga, said to the man at the vegetable stall. It was

1

market day in Blubber, the Viking village Vulgar called home. The main square was crammed with well-behaved shoppers buying things from stalls. But Vulgar longed for the bad old days – when proper Vikings looted and pillaged for their dinners!

"Buy five, get the sixth free, darlin'," said the veggie man. "Special offer, just for you, what wiv' you bein' so pretty an' that."

Vulgar almost laughed at that. *Pretty*. His mum was taller and broader than most of the men in the village. She had arms that could lift a horse, and a face that could make it run away. Vulgar had never heard anyone call her "pretty" before, not even his dad.

"Four cabbages," Helga said, glaring at the man. "And cut your nonsense."

The man gulped, nodded, then dropped four cabbages into Helga's bag. Without a word, Helga handed over a few coins, then she caught Vulgar by the arm and dragged him towards the next stall.

"Rags!" shouted another trader. "Get your rags here. Any colour you want, as long as it's grey."

"Fish heads!" cried yet another. "Lovely fish heads.

 3

Free bag of trout eyes with every purchase."

Helga made for that stall. Vulgar's mum couldn't resist a bargain – and his dad was very fond of trout eyes.

"This is *boring*," Vulgar groaned. "Why are we shopping? Real Vikings don't shop, they pillage and plunder. If it was up to me, I'd grab everything and escape in a longboat!"

A bag of trout eyes was thrust in front of Vulgar's face. He pulled back in disgust. "Well, maybe not *everything*."

Helga sighed. "Hell's teeth, I've had enough of your moaning." She took the bag of trout eyes, opened it, and tossed one in her mouth.

It made a squelchy *pop* as she bit down. "Go and take these to your father."

"Yes!" Vulgar cheered. "Where is he?"

"Cleaning the toilets."

Vulgar stopped cheering. "Oh. Do I have to?"

"Yes," snapped Helga. "Off you go. And don't stop until you get there."

Grumbling, Vulgar turned and plodded off in the direction of the Blubber public toilets. Around him, the sounds of the market continued.

"Pig tails. Git-choor curly pig tails here!"

"Earwax! Nice and gooey. Use it on your floor or use it on your beard!"

"Broadswords! Helmets! Get 'em while they're hot."

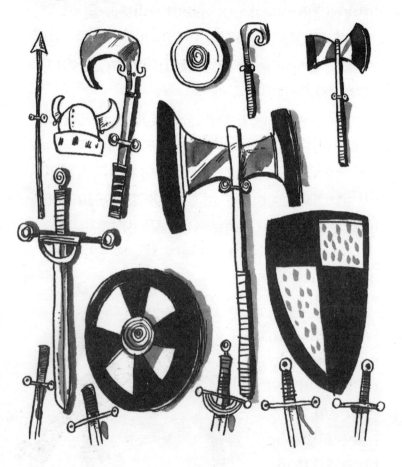

Vulgar stopped. The blacksmith's stall stood directly in front of him. Swords and

spears and axes were propped up along
the front of the stall. Helmets and shields
hung from hooks on each side. Vulgar
stared at the display, his mouth open and
his eyes wide. Suddenly shopping didn't
seem so boring after all.

The blacksmith was talking to another
customer, so he didn't notice Vulgar
running his fingers across the handles of
the swords. Vulgar gripped one with both
hands and tried to lift it, but it was
heavier than he expected. He staggered

backwards, his
knees almost
buckling, his
face turning
redder by the
second.

Eventually,
he gave up.
Straining, he
dragged the

sword back over to the stall.

Vulgar peered at his reflection in a shiny shield. Could it be? Oh yes, at last… Was his beard finally beginning to grow?

No, it was just a smudge of dirt on his cheek. Vulgar pulled a silly face and adjusted the helmet that covered his messy hair. It was dented in a few places, but then proper Viking helmets should always be dented, he thought. Dents showed a helmet had been well used.

He wasn't so keen on the horns on his

 8

helmet, if he were honest. They were small and stubby like a baby sheep's, not scary looking at all. The helmets hanging from the blacksmith's stall had *proper* horns. They curved up like mammoth tusks, pointed and sharp.

The blacksmith was still talking, so Vulgar slipped off his own helmet, pulled down a new one, and plonked it on his head.

The world went dark. The helmet was a bit on the big side. It covered most of Vulgar's face, making it impossible to see. He pushed it back a little and saw the lanky figure of his best friend, Knut, walking towards him.

Knut's helmet was even worse than Vulgar's. The horns were pointing in opposite directions, one up, one down. It looked ridiculous, but Knut never seemed all that bothered.

"All right?" Knut said, giving Vulgar a

 9

friendly grin that showed his buck teeth.

"Look at this stuff!" said Vulgar, excitedly. "Grab a helmet, quick!"

"I've got a helmet," Knut replied with a shrug.

Vulgar pulled down another new one from the stall. He tossed it to Knut. "Stick that on."

Knut changed helmets. It covered his head all the way down to his chin.

"What now?"

"Helmet war!" Vulgar cried. He lowered his helmet and charged blindly.

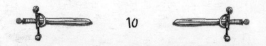

Knut ducked his head and there was a *crash* of metal as the helmets banged together.

Knut laughed. "Raging-bull attack!" he roared, as the boys locked horns again.

Suddenly, they both felt a sharp tug at the back of their tunics and they were jerked into the air. "Put the helmets down," boomed the blacksmith.

Both boys quickly removed their headgear. The blacksmith's soot-stained face snarled at them. "Now, clear off the pair of you," he said, dropping them into the mud and taking the helmets from their hands.

"That was fun," Vulgar said with a grin, as he and Knut shuffled away from the stall.

"What do you want to do now?" asked Knut.

Vulgar shrugged. "I've got to take these trout eyes to my dad."

Knut licked his lips. "I love trout eyes. Can I have one?"

"Yeah, if you want," said Vulgar. He held the bag out to his friend, but another hand snatched it out of his.

"Mmm, trout eyes," sneered a bigger boy. "You shouldn't have!"

"Hey, give those back, Gunnar," Vulgar yelped.

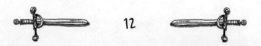

Gunnar the Grim was Vulgar's arch-enemy from the neighbouring village of Gulp. He enjoyed nothing more than making Vulgar's life miserable.

"Yum," Gunnar said with a grin, stuffing a handful of the eyes into his mouth. "Delicious."

Vulgar tried to snatch the bag back, but Gunnar held them up out of his reach.

"Give them back," Vulgar snarled. "They're for my dad."

"Oh, that's his reward for cleaning the bogs, is it?" the bigger boy laughed. "Here, you can have them."

There was a soggy *splat* as Gunnar tipped the entire bag over Vulgar's head. "See you around, *stinky*," he sniggered, then he strode off through the market.

"You OK?" asked Knut, helping his friend up.

13

Vulgar wiped off the worst of the trout eyes and glared at Gunnar's back. "That does it," he growled. He searched the ground until he found something to throw. It was a mouldy, rotten potato. The perfect weapon. "He asked for this."

Taking careful aim, Vulgar hurled the rotting spud at Gunnar. "Yes..." he said, as the potato flew towards the Gulp boy's head.

At the last moment, Gunnar turned away, revealing Princess Freya standing by the jewellery stall, admiring the gold and silver.

"No..." Vulgar groaned, as the soggy spud struck with a *SPLAT* and exploded against the side of Freya's head.

The princess cried out in shock, her long, blonde plaits whipping round as she turned in Vulgar's direction. Her eyes narrowed with rage. Her fists clenched. Vulgar felt Knut take cover behind him.

"Now you've done it," Knut whimpered. "She'll get us locked up!" He took another look at her face. "Or maybe just kill us."

Before Freya could do either of those things, the blast of a horn stopped her.

Around the market the buyers stopped buying and the sellers stopped selling, and everyone turned in the direction of the noise.

As he waited to hear the announcement that the horn blast heralded, Vulgar hoped with all of his heart that it would be exciting enough to make Freya forget about the potato!

CHAPTER TWO

THE BIG ANNOUNCEMENT

The sound had come from the direction of the Great Hall, which stood in the centre of the village square, just at the edge of the market itself.

As the noise of the horn faded, an elderly Viking with a crooked walking stick shuffled to the top of the steps. It was Harrumf, steward of the Great Hall.

"Right then," he began, then he

coughed uncontrollably for several
seconds. Everyone gathered
around to watch as the old
man hacked and
spluttered, turning
redder and redder
in the face.

He shook his
head and muttered
below his breath before
continuing. "Pray
silence," he said, even though no
one in the crowd had said a word, "for
the Master of Disaster, the Regal Eagle,
your *Right Royal-tastic Ruler*, the one, the
only..."

"Oh, get on with it," whispered a voice
from somewhere behind Harrumf.

"King Olaf," said the old man, flatly.
There was a faint smattering of applause
as he shuffled off, then much louder
clapping as King Olaf waddled out,

18

preceded by his enormous belly.

"Friends," he began in his deep, booming voice. "Do you know what day it is?"

"Market day," said a voice from the crowd.

King Olaf shook his head. "Nope."

"Yes it is," insisted the voice.

"Well, yes, I mean *obviously* it's market day," Olaf said.

"Then why did you say it wasn't?" someone demanded.

King Olaf sighed. "No, it isn't... I mean..." He took a deep breath. "Look, I know it's market day. We all know it's market day. But what *else* is today?"

There was silence from the crowd.

"Tuesday?"

"No," said Olaf. "Well, I mean, *yes*, OK, it's Tuesday. But what's so special about this Tuesday? That's what I'm trying to get at."

He cast his gaze across the crowd. A sea of puzzled faces looked back at him. "Think about it," he said. He was still smiling, but it was becoming more and more strained. "What's due to happen two days from now? Hmm?"

A hand shot up in the front row. Olaf nodded encouragingly down at a skinny man with a wispy red beard. "Yes?"

"Thursday."

"The Games," King Olaf snapped, his smile finally falling away completely. "In two days, it's the Great Gulp Games!"

A murmur passed through the crowd. The Great Gulp Games. Was it that time of year already?

"As you know, every year one athlete from Blubber and one athlete from Gulp compete in the Games. The winning village gets possession of the Skull Cup."

There was an "*Ooooh*" from the crowd as Harrumf held up the trophy. It was a

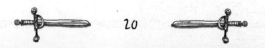

huge drinking cup with a magnificent skull etched on to its side. Vulgar's eyes locked on to it. It was the greatest thing he'd ever seen in his entire life!

"And, of course, there will be the traditional winner's feast." There was a rumbling from the villagers' stomachs. "For the past ten years an athlete from the village of Gulp has won the Games. Will this year be different?"

"Doubt it," snorted Gunnar from the front of the crowd. Vulgar's eyes narrowed, but he kept listening to the king.

"There will be five events," Olaf continued. "Walrus wrestling, ice swimming, goat hurdling, reindeer racing and, of course,

Thor's hammer throw. It will take strength and courage. Only the bravest Vikings stand any chance of victory.

"So, who will step forward?" asked the king. "Who will take part in this year's Games?"

The crowd remained silent.

"Will no one volunteer?" asked Olaf. "Is no one brave enough?"

"Crazy enough, you mean," muttered someone near the back.

"Yeah," agreed another voice. "Swimming through ice? Fighting a walrus?

You'd have to be mad!"

Olaf pointed to Knut. "How about you, young man?"

Knut looked nervously at the people around him. "What, me?"

"Yes! Do you have what it takes to win the Games for Blubber?"

Knut shrank back and stammered, "I, um, can't."

King Olaf frowned. "Why not?"

"I've broken my legs."

The king and most of the crowd stared at Knut's legs. "They don't look broken."

"No, but they are," Knut insisted. "Ouch," he added, as if to prove his point.

Gunnar elbowed Vulgar sharply in the ribs. "Is that the best your village has got?" he sniggered. "You'd better start praying to Odin, because you're going to need a miracle."

Vulgar knew he was right. Blubber

 23

hadn't won the Games since his mum had retired. Helga had been the greatest walrus wrestler the Viking world had ever seen, but was forced to step down when the walruses started refusing to fight her.

"No volunteers so far," Olaf announced. "Does no one have what it takes?"

"Me," said Gunnar, stepping forward. He pulled a face at Vulgar and laughed. "I'm stronger and faster than anyone in Blubber."

Right, that did it. Vulgar

 24

had had enough of Gunnar's insults. It was time to show everyone that there was at least one real Viking left in Blubber!

"And me!" Vulgar said, raising his hand.

"Are you *crazy*?" gasped Knut.

"Champions run in my family," Vulgar whispered. "Unless you'd rather do it?"

Knut thought for a moment, then clapped his friend on the shoulder and smiled encouragingly. "Good luck."

"Very well," boomed King Olaf. "We have our athletes! In two days the annual Great Gulp Games begin!"

Bowing deeply, Olaf waddled back into the Great Hall. Harrumf took his place and scowled down at the crowd. "Right, that's it. Now clear off, the lot of you."

Almost immediately, the sounds of the market started up again. Vulgar and Knut turned to go, but Freya blocked the way.

"So," she sniffed. "You think you can win the Great Gulp Games, do you?"

"Of course!" said Vulgar. "Like mother, like son!"

"You're just going to make a fool of yourself," Freya told him.

"No, I won't!"

"Yes, you will. Unless I help you."

Vulgar snorted. "How?"

"I can train you," Freya replied. "I'll be your coach."

"No chance," Vulgar said. "I don't need anyone to coach me, especially not a girl."

Freya shrugged and stepped aside. "Fair enough," she said. "Then I'll just have to tell my dad that you threw rotten vegetables at me. I doubt he'll let you take part in the Games after that. You probably won't even get to watch, as you'll be locked up in the dungeon."

"You wouldn't!" said Vulgar.

26

Knut nodded. "She would."

Freya smiled sweetly. "So," she said, "what's it to be? Do you want to win the Skull Cup or not?"

"Yes," Vulgar sighed.

"Yes *what?*"

Vulgar gritted his teeth. "Yes, *coach.*"

"There, that wasn't so hard, was it?" Freya beamed. "Now go home and get some rest." She cracked her knuckles and smiled wickedly. "Because tomorrow is Training Day!"

CHAPTER THREE

TRAINING DAY

Vulgar lay curled up under his blanket,
dreaming of longboats and sea monsters.
He sat up suddenly when something
bounced off his forehead. Blinking away
sleep, he didn't notice a second pebble
flying in through the open shutters of his
window until it hit him on the shoulder
with a *thud*.

"Hey!" he yelped, leaping out of bed.

The stone floor was cold beneath his feet as he crossed to the window. He ducked as another pebble came hurtling through.

"What are you doing?" he shouted.

Freya was standing outside. She had swapped her usual fancy gown for a pair of long shorts and a sleeveless tabard. Knut was standing beside her, looking half asleep.

"Waking you up," Freya replied. "It's time to start training."

She hurled another stone at him. It struck him on the head and went *clunk*.

"Ow! Cut it out, I'm awake!"

"I know," Freya said with a cheeky grin. "I just like throwing stones at you."

Muttering, Vulgar turned from the window and hurried out of his bedroom, pulling on his clothes as he went. There were a few slices of stale bread on the kitchen table. He picked one up and stuffed it in his mouth, then pulled open the front door of the hut. Grunt, his shaggy old wolfhound, followed him out of the kitchen, then slumped down again on the front path and immediately started snoring.

"How do you feel?" Freya asked Vulgar. "Wide awake?"

"Not really," said Vulgar.

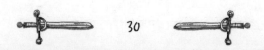

Knut groaned. "I know the feeling. I don't even know what I'm doing here."

"You're assistant coach, remember?" Freya sighed. "I've told you a hundred times."

"Have you?" Knut said. He yawned. "I wasn't listening."

Freya shook her head, then turned to Vulgar. If Vulgar was going to have any chance of winning, she explained, he would need all the practice he could get. That was why she had come up with the perfect training plan that would turn him from a nobody into a champion.

"But I'm not a nobody!" Vulgar complained.

"Yes, you are," Freya said. "But you won't be for long. First up, hammer throwing. Knut, the hammer please."

Knut looked blankly at her. "What?"

"The hammer," Freya repeated, snapping her fingers. She glared at him.

"You did bring the hammer, didn't you?"

"I didn't know I was supposed to bring a hammer," Knut said with a shrug. "You didn't tell me."

"I did so! Yesterday. I said, 'Bring a hammer, don't forget'."

Knut shrugged his shoulders. "I guess I didn't hear you."

Freya sighed. "Right. So we don't have a hammer. That's a great start."

"So can I just go back to bed, then?" asked Vulgar.

"No, you cannot. You'll just have to throw something else," Freya snapped. She looked at the ground around them, then pointed to something a few metres away. "There. Throw that."

"That?" said Vulgar. "But that's a stick."

"So? A hammer's just a stick, too."

"With a big heavy bit on the end," Vulgar reminded her.

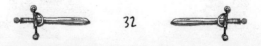

Freya sniffed. "Well, this is the best we can do. Get throwing."

"Good luck," said Knut.

"Um... thanks," said Vulgar. He bent to pick up the stick, but a shout from Freya stopped him.

"Bend at the knees," she told him. "You should always keep your back straight when lifting heavy weights."

"Heavy weights? But it's a stick."

"No, it isn't. It's a hammer," Freya said, and the way she glared at him almost made Vulgar believe her. "Now pick it up and throw it. And don't forget to bend at the knees."

Vulgar hesitated. Then he bent at the knees and picked up the stick. It was little more than a twig, really, and didn't weigh very much at all. He flipped it over in his hand a few times, then flicked his wrist and send the stick whizzing through the air.

Knut clapped enthusiastically. "Well done, Vulgar. That went for miles."

Freya wasn't impressed. "That's your hammer-throwing technique?"

"No, it's my stick-throwing technique," Vulgar said.

Freya handed him another stick. It weighed even less than the first one. "I want to see you spinning on the spot," she said. "Like you're throwing a proper

34

hammer. Spin five times, then let go.
Let's see how far it goes then."

"OK," said Vulgar with a shrug. He
took the stick and held it as he would a
real hammer. He began to
turn, slowly at
first, then faster
and faster.

By the fourth spin Vulgar began to feel
dizzy. By the fifth spin he felt sick, and
by the sixth he'd lost count of how many
spins he'd done. He decided to let go.

The stick flew from his grip. It rocketed towards Freya and Knut, and they barely managed to duck out of the way in time. They all watched the stick sail through the window of Vulgar's kitchen. There was a *crash* and an angry cry of "Ouch!".

"Oops," said Knut.

"Sorry, Mum!" shouted Vulgar. He turned to Freya. "Maybe we should try something less dangerous?"

Freya thought about this. "Or how about something *more* dangerous? Walrus wrestling!"

"Before you even say it," began Knut, "no one told me to bring a walrus."

"We're not using a *real* walrus!" sighed Freya. "We're using something else."

"Another stick?" asked Vulgar, hopefully.

"Not exactly," replied Freya. She reached into a fold in her clothing and pulled out a string of sausages. She whistled loudly. Grunt lifted his head. He saw the sausages and licked his chops. "Dried elk sausages," said Freya, shoving them down the back of Vulgar's tunic. "Come get them!"

Vulgar had never seen Grunt move so quickly. The flea-bitten dog was on him in four big leaps, licking him with his rough tongue and snuffling at his neck with his cold, wet nose.

"Ah, Grunt, get off!" cried Vulgar as he fell backwards on to the ground. Grunt's paws had him pinned, and the dog's sandpaper tongue was licking months' worth of dirt off Vulgar's face.

"Well, wrestle him then!" said Freya. "Come on, go for a headlock!"

But Vulgar was trapped beneath Grunt and completely helpless. He began to laugh as the dog's hairy snout snuffled around the back of his neck.

"Stop it, that tickles!" With a yelp of delight, Grunt pulled the string of sausages free. He barked happily, then trotted off back along the path, carrying his prize with him.

Vulgar looked up to find Freya scowling down at him.

"Pathetic," she sighed.

 39

"I'd like to see you do any better," said Vulgar. "What's next?"

"Ice swimming," said Freya.

"Where are we going to practise that? The duck pond?"

Freya shook her head. "Not cold enough."

Vulgar went to sit up, but Freya stopped him. "Don't move," she said. "Knut. The bucket."

Knut appeared beside her, a large wooden bucket in his hands. Vulgar looked up at his friend and frowned. "Knut? What's going on?"

"I'm sorry, Vulgar," Knut shrugged. "She's making me do this."

"But I'm your best friend!"

"Yeah, but she's scarier than you are," said Knut. Then he tipped the bucket and what felt like an entire ocean's worth of freezing cold water landed on Vulgar's head.

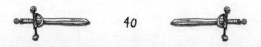

40

Vulgar opened his mouth to scream, but the sound froze somewhere in his throat. He jumped to his feet and began running in circles, patting himself as he tried to warm up.

"C-cold,"
he whimpered.
"S-s-so c-c-cold!"

"Don't be such a crybaby," Freya told him. "It's time to practise reindeer racing."

"H-how?" Vulgar stammered, still shivering. "We don't have a reindeer, and I'm not riding on Grunt."

Freya grinned. "No. I've got a better idea."

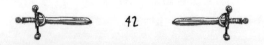

"Faster, Vulgar, faster! You'll never win at this rate."

"It's not my fault," Vulgar said. "It's this reindeer. It's too slow."

"Yeah, well, you're too heavy, you know?" wheezed Knut. He was crawling along on his hands and knees with Vulgar perched on his back. "I don't see why I have to be the reindeer," he complained to Freya. "Why can't you do it?"

Freya laughed. "Because one of us is a princess, and one of us isn't. Now stop talking and giddy-up."

Muttering, Knut began to hurry forward. Vulgar gave a yelp of surprise as he lost his balance. He flailed his arms wildly for a moment, then fell off Knut's back with a *splash* – right into a puddle of the icy water Knut had poured over his head.

"Right, I've had enough," cried Vulgar. "Training Day is over."

"If you don't practise you won't win," said Freya.

"If I *do* practise any more, I won't be able to walk tomorrow!" replied Vulgar.

Freya folded her arms crossly. "You're not going anywhere until you've practised goat hurdling."

"OK," Vulgar agreed. "Watch this."

With one great leap, Vulgar bounded over the wall into his garden.

44

"There," he said, "practice over." Then he raced along his path and into his house, slamming the door behind him.

CHAPTER FOUR
TROLL ROLLING

Next morning, Vulgar sat at the kitchen table. His mum was making a fuss.

"A champion's breakfast, that's what you need," she announced, ruffling his hair as she placed a bowl down in front of him.

Vulgar stared at the thick grey liquid, and the browny-black lumps that lurked just below the surface. He picked up a

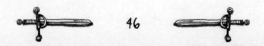

spoon and prodded the food suspiciously.
The gloopy fluid went *blurp* and the
room suddenly smelled like a donkey's
trump.

"What's this?"

"Whale meat," Helga said. "*Rancid*
whale meat in cod liver oil. It's what I
always ate before the Games."

Vulgar's scrawny dad, Harald, took
a seat across from his son. He smiled
encouragingly. "It'll put hairs on your
chest," he said. "Like it did for your
mother."

"I remember my first Games," Helga said, joining them at the table. "They had different events back then, of course. Remember the troll rolling?"

"Do I remember the troll rolling?" Harald laughed. "How could I forget? They never did find out where that one stopped, did they?"

Helga smiled proudly. "Iceland, they reckoned, but they couldn't be sure."

"Happy days," said Harald, squeezing

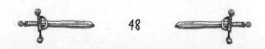

his wife's hand.

"Happy days," agreed Helga.

"Not for the troll by the sounds of things," mumbled Vulgar. He held his nose and slid a lump of whale meat into his mouth, then swallowed it without chewing. "Yum," he lied, standing up. "Time to go."

Helga threw her arms around her son and pulled him in close. It was like being hugged by a mountain. "Good luck, Vulgar," she said. "But remember, it's not the winning that matters, it's the taking part. We're proud of you, win or lose."

"Thanks, Mum," he said.

His mum smiled. "But obviously we'd prefer it if you won."

Vulgar stood at the entrance to Bragi's field, where most of the events would be taking place. A large crowd had already gathered, and it was chatting excitedly.

In the athletes' area, Gunnar was warming up. He was down on the grass, doing one-armed push-ups.

"One… two…" He saw Vulgar watching him. "Three million

and five… three million and six…"

"So, still think you can beat Gunnar?" asked Knut as he joined his friend.

"Easy peasy," Vulgar said, jogging on the spot.

50

Knut nodded. "He *is* quite strong, though."

"So am I," said Vulgar, flexing his arm muscles, or where they would be if he had any.

"And he can run really fast," Knut added.

"Yes, thanks, I know all that!" said Vulgar, touching his toes. "You're supposed to be cheering me on."

Knut frowned. "Am I? Oh, well… Forget everything I just said, then."

 51

Across the field, Freya spotted Vulgar and hurried over to join him. "You ready?" she asked. "Why aren't you getting warmed up?"

"I am," said Vulgar. "Don't get your tunic in a twist."

Freya backed away in disgust. "Ugh, your breath stinks. What have you been eating?"

"Rancid whale meat," Vulgar explained. "My mum made me."

"Yuck," muttered Freya, then she shoved him to the ground. "Push-ups," she barked. "Give me twenty."

Vulgar snorted. "No problem," he said, pushing himself up. His arms shook for a second, then gave way completely. He landed face down on the grass.

"One," sighed Freya, waiting for Vulgar to get up. He didn't.

A loud fanfare signalled the beginning of the opening ceremony. The two athletes gathered together in front of a raised wooden platform, with the audience crowding around behind them.

"Blubber and Gulp," said King Olaf, addressing the crowd. "We are gathered here in the eyes of Odin and Thor and Bragi and…" He waved a hand in a vague circle. "Um… er… you know, for the eighteenth annual Great Gulp Games!"

A cheer rose up from the crowd. Vulgar glanced across at Gunnar. The boy from Gulp stuck his tongue out and smirked at Vulgar.

"As you know, the Games began as a way to encourage friendly competition between Viking villages in times of peace. Gulp was host to that first competition and the village gave it its name." The king cleared his throat importantly. "I remember my first Games," he said, rocking back on his heels. "And my first throw of Thor's hammer. Why, I threw it so hard it travelled all the way around the Earth and landed just a few feet behind me!"

"I heard you just threw it in the wrong

 55

direction," muttered a voice in the crowd.

"But enough about me," said Olaf. "It's time for new champions to prove themselves. It's time for new legends to be made. It's time…" Olaf drew in a deep breath and held his arms out to the side. "… for the Games to begin!'

King Olaf looked directly down at the athletes. "May the best Viking win," he said.

"Oh, don't worry," said Gunnar and Vulgar at the same time. "I will."

CHAPTER FIVE

THE GAMES BEGIN

Harrumf took his seat at the announcer's table and noisily cleared his throat.

"First up it's Thor's 'ammer throw," he said, speaking into a bull's horn. "The winner's the one wot chucks it the furthest. Gunnar the Grim to throw first. Let's see if he can show that 'ammer who's boss."

Gunnar strolled casually over to where

 57

the hammer lay, waving to the crowd as he walked. He tried to pick up the hammer, but no longer looked quite so confident. His eyes nearly bulging out of his head, Gunnar grunted and heaved

the huge metal mallet through the air. With a loud THUNK it plopped to the ground about a metre in front of him.

"That was more like Thor's hammer drop," Vulgar whispered to Knut.

"Wait, that was just a practice go," whined Gunnar.

"That's yer lot," said Harrumf. "It's Vulgar's turn." Gunnar stomped over to the hammer and dragged it back to the starting line.

He seemed to be rubbing it clean for
Vulgar.

"Here you are," said Gunnar with a sly
grin. "All *shiny* and new."

"You can do this," Freya
encouraged Vulgar.
"Send that hammer all
the way to Valhalla."

Vulgar nodded,
then reached down for
the hammer. He straightened up quickly
but his hands slid off the handle and
Vulgar fell on his bottom. A low giggle
passed through the Gulp half of the
audience and the Blubber fans pelted
them with stale rock
cakes. Vulgar struggled
to his feet and grabbed
the handle again, but it
kept slipping out of
his hands.

Finally, he managed

to get a grip on the hammer. His muscles straining with the effort, he heaved it up to his shoulder and the hammer slipped out of his hands and fell on his foot.

"Yow!" yelped Vulgar, hopping up and down.

"Ooh," said Knut, hurrying over to check on his friend. "I bet that hurt."

Freya stormed up to Vulgar. "What's going on? Why didn't you throw it? He's ahead now."

"The handle was slippery," Vulgar said, wiping his hands on his crumpled leather tunic. "I think he put grease on it."

"An' it looks like the first event goes to Gulp," announced Harrumf, "on

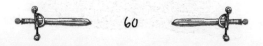

60

account of Vulgar not being able to pick the 'ammer up properly, never mind throw it. Next up, walrus wrestlin'."

Gunnar nudged Vulgar as they began the walk over to the walrus pen. "Nice work, stinky. Can you feel victory *slipping* away?"

There was a cheer and a *splat* and a wet walrus landed on the grass in front of them.

Gunnar leapt on to it, wrapping his arms around its chubby neck. The animal bucked and twisted, throwing the boy off. Gunnar lunged at the walrus again and again, but just kept bouncing off its rubbery body.

As Gunnar tried to tackle the walrus one more time, the beast lowered its head and…

RIIIIIPPP!

The walrus's tusks tore a big hole in Gunnar's shorts. As the crowd howled with laughter, Gunnar held his bottom and circled the walrus. Vulgar watched closely. All Gunnar had to do was flip the animal on to its back, then it would be Vulgar's turn. Whoever flipped the walrus the fastest would be the winner. Vulgar just had to hope that it took Gunnar a long time to—

Ding-ding. Harrumf rang a bell as a furious Gunnar slammed a shoulder into the walrus, rolling it over on to its back. The Gulp fans roared with delight.

"Gunnar one, walrus nuffink," announced Harrumf. "Time, one minute forty-two seconds. Vulgar up next."

63

The Blubber villagers cheered as
Vulgar got into position opposite the
walrus. Loudest of all was Helga. "Come
on, my brave boy!" she hollered.

"Mu-um!" winced Vulgar, turning to
face his opponent. He stared at its sharp
tusks and tried not
to think about
how dangerous
they looked.

But he was the son of a walrus-wrestling champion, after all. He *owned* this event!

It just looked so *big*, like a giant slug with a bushy white moustache, and horns sticking out of its face. When it came to wrestling, Vulgar's usual technique was to trip his opponent up and make them fall over, but the walrus was already lying on the ground. It had nowhere left to fall.

Ding-ding. Harrumf rang the bell and Vulgar mounted an attack. He wrapped an arm around the walrus's squidgy body and squeezed.

The walrus yawned.

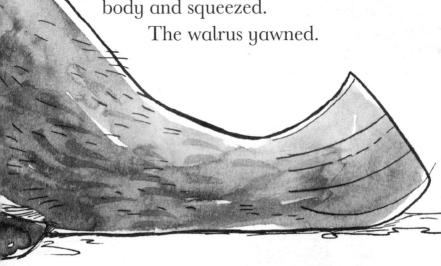

Vulgar turned and tried to poke his elbows into the animal's ribs. But he wasn't sure if a walrus even had ribs, never mind where in its body they were, so he gave up on that move quite quickly.

"Come on, Vulgar," shouted Freya. "Stop tickling it!"

Vulgar felt his cheeks go red. He hurled himself at the walrus for a third time, trying to roll it over on to its broad back.

The walrus pushed back, nudging him with its smooth head. Vulgar fell backwards on to the ground, and suddenly the animal was looming over him, its face just a few centimetres from his.

"Get off," Vulgar yelped, but the yelp became a laugh as he felt the walrus's fuzzy moustache on his cheeks. "S-stop it," he giggled. "Cut it out!"

A strange expression passed over the

animal's face. It sniffed the air. Then it
sniffed Vulgar's
breath and
gave a loud,
excited *bark*.
It sat
down, its
tongue
hanging
out, and
clapped its
front flippers together.

Vulgar breathed into his hand and
smelled it. His breath still reeked of rotten
whale meat.

That must be it, Vulgar thought. *The
walrus likes the smell of rancid whale!*

To test the idea, he blew a puff of
breath right in the animal's face. The
walrus gave another happy *bark* then
rolled over on to its back.

Ding-ding went the bell.

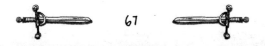

"What?" yelled Gunnar. "That doesn't count, he didn't touch it."

"Walrus down," Harrumf said. "Time, one minute forty-one seconds."

"Yes!" cried Freya, leaping up and punching the air. "You beat him by one second!"

"That's my boy!" Helga cheered. She picked up her husband and hugged him. Harald's eyes almost popped out of his head.

"Second round goes to Vulgar," announced Harrumf.

He carried on talking, but the words were drowned out by the cheers of the Blubber crowd crying, "Vulgar! Vulgar! Vulgar!"

It was neck and neck, and with three rounds left there was everything to play for.

CHAPTER SIX

RUN REINDEER RUN

Vulgar had never ridden a reindeer before. He wasn't quite sure where you held on but the antlers were as good a place as any, he guessed.

The reindeer he sat on was light grey with drooping shoulders and sad eyes. Beside him, Gunnar straddled his reindeer. Gunnar's reindeer was so dark it was almost black. It stomped the

 69

ground with its powerful legs and blew steam from its wide nostrils. Vulgar's reindeer just munched the grass.

"Even a bolt of Thor's lightning won't make that old nag gallop," said Gunnar, annoyingly.

Not for the first time since climbing on it, Vulgar wondered if he'd chosen the wrong reindeer. There was no time to worry about that now, though. Harrumf stood at the starting line beside them.

"All the way around the course an' back here," he told them. "No shortcuts,

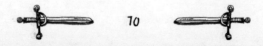

no funny stuff. Anyone falls off, an'
they're disquaffilied… dequalifiled…
defollicled." He shook his head. "Forget
it. Anyone falls off, an' they're *out*."

"You can win this, Vulgar," shouted
Freya from the spectators' area.

"Don't fall off and get trampled,"
added Knut.

Harrumf cupped his hands around his
mouth. "Bang!" he shouted, and both
reindeer shot forward. Or rather,
Gunnar's reindeer shot forward. Vulgar's
sauntered slowly for seven or eight
metres, then stopped to nibble a patch of
grass.

Vulgar looked along the track. Gunnar
was charging ahead, hanging on to his
reindeer's antlers for dear life.

"He's getting away," yelped Vulgar.
The reindeer ignored him and kept
chewing.

"Move!" bellowed Freya, and suddenly

the animal bucked and leapt into life. It raced forward, forcing Vulgar to cling tightly to its neck. Terrified of the screaming girl behind it, the reindeer was soon matching the speed of the one in front. But Gunnar had a big head start.

They thundered across the field, then out on to the path that led around the pond. The cheering of the crowd sounded a long way away.

"Can't you go any faster?" asked Vulgar. The reindeer didn't change its pace. Then Vulgar had a brainwave. "You like vegetables, right?" he said.

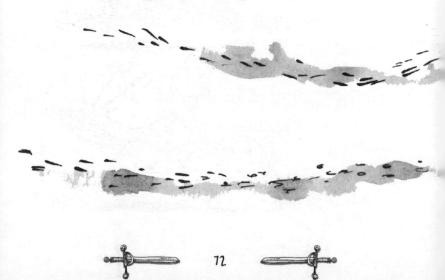

"I'll make you a deal. If you speed up, I'll give you all my vegetables for the rest of my life."

Vulgar wasn't sure if the animal understood him, but he felt the reindeer's stomach rumble and it began to run faster. Its hooves beat against the ground like a drum, and Vulgar had to hold on tight to avoid being blown off its back.

Vulgar pulled up alongside Gunnar. "Oh, Loki here! I've caught you up," said Vulgar.

"Oh no you haven't," shrieked Gunnar.
The boy from Gulp leaned over, pulled
off Vulgar's helmet, and dropped it over
his reindeer's ears.

"Whoa!" cried Vulgar, as his reindeer
lost control and ran off the path. With
the helmet covering its eyes, the reindeer
blundered through a row of
gardens, trampling carrots
and tearing up cabbages

as it went. And then, suddenly and
without warning, it stopped. Vulgar was
catapulted off the animal's back. He
flapped his arms like a bird as he sailed
through the air, hoping he could learn

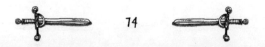

how to fly. He couldn't, though, and he landed with a *splat* in a large heap of smelly elk manure.

Ten minutes later, Vulgar walked the final few steps into Bragi's field, where he found the crowd waiting for him, holding their noses. In the distance, he could see a terrified Gunnar still clinging on to his reindeer, which had crossed the finishing line and decided to keep on going.

 75

"Hard luck," said Freya sympathetically. "But when you fall off a reindeer, you've just got to get back on again."

Knut shook his head. "Actually, it's goat hurdling next, so he'd better not."

"Point to Gulp, on account of Vulgar being disquafillied," announced Harrumf. "Gulp lead two points to one," the old man said, pulling a disgusted face. "Now would someone get that boy some soap."

When most of the manure had been scrubbed away, Vulgar hurried back over to Freya and Knut.

"Gunnar keeps cheating! I'm not going

to let him get away with it!" he fumed.

"That's the spirit – you show him what Blubberers are made of," said Freya.

"Er, blubber?" suggested Knut helpfully.

"No," said Freya impatiently. "I mean Vulgar's going to win the goat hurdling."

"Yeah!" shouted Vulgar. "Real Vikings NEVER give up!"

"But what if Gunnar cheats again?" asked Knut.

"Don't worry, I'll think of something," muttered Freya darkly.

"It's time to lock horns again," announced Harrumph. He pointed over to the edge of the field. "Take your places for the goat hurdling!"

Vulgar jogged across to the starting line. After his impressive hurdle over the garden wall during training yesterday, he was feeling confident. How much harder could it be to hurdle a few goats?

 77

"Pee-yew!" sniffed Gunnar. "Did you stand in something, Vulgar?"

"You're just a cheater," retorted Vulgar.

"A cheetah? The fastest animal on Earth? Why, yes, then I am a cheetah," said Gunnar with a smirk.

"Bang!" shouted Harrumf again, and both boys began to run.

The rules of the event were simple. There were twenty goats grazing on the hill beside Bragi's field. Both competitors had to leap over every one of the goats, run to the top of the hill, then run back down. The first one to reach the finish line would be the winner.

They were neck and neck as they hurdled the first goat. It blinked lazily, then went back to chewing the grass. They cleared the second goat at the same time, and the third, and the fourth.

As Vulgar got ready to leap the fifth

goat, he tripped on a rock. Knocked off balance, Vulgar fell clumsily. He landed with an *Oof* on the goat's back.

Gunnar hooted with laughter and said, "Guess you were *kidding* when you said you were going to win!"

Startled, the goat began to charge. As Vulgar was bounced along on its back, he looked ahead in the direction the animal was running. There was Gunnar, racing on. There was Gunnar's bottom, dead ahead. And there were the goat's horns, quickly closing the gap.

THONK!

"AAAAARGH!"

The goat's horns rammed into Gunnar's backside and the boy fell flat on his face. Vulgar hopped from the goat's back in time to see a screaming Gunnar rolling all the way back down the hill. As Gunnar reached the bottom, Vulgar saw Freya and Knut jumping up and down with delight.

Laughing, Vulgar hurdled his way up the hill. He was still chuckling a few minutes later when he ran back to the field to the sound of clapping and cheering.

"That wasn't fair," Gunnar growled.

"Yeah." Vulgar grinned. "You really got a *bum deal*."

"Two points each," announced Harrumf. "It all comes down to this final event."

The old man pointed out to sea, past the frozen fjords to the dark water beyond. "Let the ice swim begin!"

CHAPTER SEVEN

THE GRAND FINAL

Vulgar stood on the ice, trying to rub some heat into his bare arms. He was wearing a pair of swimming trunks that Helga had made from an old sack, and he felt colder than he had ever felt in his life. And he was about to get colder still.

Harrumf stepped on to the ice, slid, and landed on his back. He didn't even bother trying to get up.

 83

"First one to make it all the way to the rock and back is the winner," he said, pointing vaguely in the direction of a small island out in the middle of the bay.

"It has been a fine Games," said King Olaf, joining them on the ice. "Good lu-uuuuk!"

There was a *thud* as King Olaf landed on the ground beside his steward.

"Ready!" cried Harrumf.

Vulgar looked across at Gunnar. The bigger boy grinned back at him. For a moment, Vulgar thought he smelled something. Something he recognised...

"Steady!"

Cheers went up from both sides of the crowd.

"For the glory of Gulp!" cried one of Gunnar's fans.

"You can do it, Gunnar," bellowed another.

"Try not to drown, Vulgar!" said Knut.

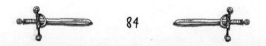

The smell was still bothering Vulgar. It was fishy, like... like...

He let out a gasp. *The rotten cheat!*

"Go!"

Both boys dived into the water. The cold hit Vulgar like a million pinpricks. He tried to breathe, but his lungs weren't working, so he thrashed wildly in the water just trying to stay afloat. Meanwhile, Gunnar was powering away, cutting through the waves like a shark.

Whale blubber. That was the smell. Gunnar had rubbed whale blubber on to his skin to trap his body heat inside. No wonder he didn't seem to be feeling the cold. He'd cheated. *Again.*

But Vulgar refused to give up. Kicking his shaking legs, he front-crawled away from the shore, and set off in hot pursuit – or *cold* pursuit, at least – of the cheater from Gulp.

Vulgar was a strong swimmer. Only

Freya was normally able to keep up with him. But the cold was making his muscles seize up, and Gunnar was pulling further and further away with every stroke.

Over the sound of the cheering, Vulgar heard a loud *splash*. Freya screamed, and both competitors stopped swimming and looked towards the shore.

"Polar bear!" shrieked the princess. She pointed to a large, hairy shape in the water. It was swimming in their direction.

 86

And it was swimming fast.

Gunnar squealed and began thrashing towards the halfway rock. Vulgar began to swim, too, ignoring the cold. He reached the rock in less than a minute. Gunnar was trying to scramble up the rock, but the blubber on his skin meant he kept sliding back down into the sea.

Vulgar looked over his shoulder and got a good look at the polar bear, which was now only a few metres behind him.

It was smaller than he'd expected. It wasn't white, either, more a sort of yellowy brown. It reminded him almost

 87

exactly of...

Grunt! It wasn't a polar bear at all, it was his dog, Grunt!

Of course, there was no way he was going to tell Gunnar that.

Gritting his teeth in determination, Vulgar swam around the rock and began to race back towards the shore. The "polar bear" swam alongside him, wagging its soggy tail happily, and occasionally going, "Woof."

Glancing over his shoulder, Vulgar could see Gunnar jumping up and down

on the rock, waving his fists in anger and shouting that he'd been tricked.

A cheer went up from the Blubber crowd, as Vulgar finally pulled himself up on to solid ground and stumbled over the finish line.

"Congratulations, my boy!" boomed King Olaf. A blanket was draped over Vulgar's shoulders and the Skull Cup was thrust into his shivering hands. "Blubber is the winner of this year's Games!"

The loudest cheer of all came from
Helga. She hoisted her son into the air
and sat him on her shoulders, showing
him off proudly to
the crowds.

"You did it!"
she said.

"With a little help from Grunt," replied
Vulgar.

Freya looked up at him and smiled
innocently. "Grunt?" she said. "Silly me,
I thought it was a polar bear."

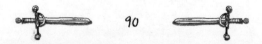

Vulgar grinned. "No, you didn't," he whispered.

"No," admitted Freya. "I didn't."

"Well done to both brave competitors," boomed King Olaf. "Now come and shake hands like true Vikings."

Vulgar cheerfully offered his hand to Gunnar, who had finally swum back from the rock. "Whale *blubber* is no match for Vikings from *Blubber*," he whispered.

Glowering, the boy from Gulp gave Vulgar a very cold, wet handshake.

"The victor's feast will be held tonight," announced Olaf. This was met by even more cheering. "And as victor, Vulgar will have a very special honour."

Vulgar's eyes went wide with excitement. What was it going to be? Would he be presented with another prize? A broadsword, maybe? Or a new helmet?

"He shall have the honour," continued

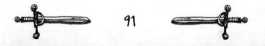

Olaf, "of dancing all night long with my daughter, Princess Freya!"

Vulgar's face fell. Freya winked at him, and grinned. Somewhere in the crowd, Vulgar heard Knut laughing.

Up on his mum's shoulders, Vulgar let out a low groan.

Dancing.

With Freya.

All night!

Maybe victory wasn't so sweet, after all.